SPLAT!
What's that?

Buster Books

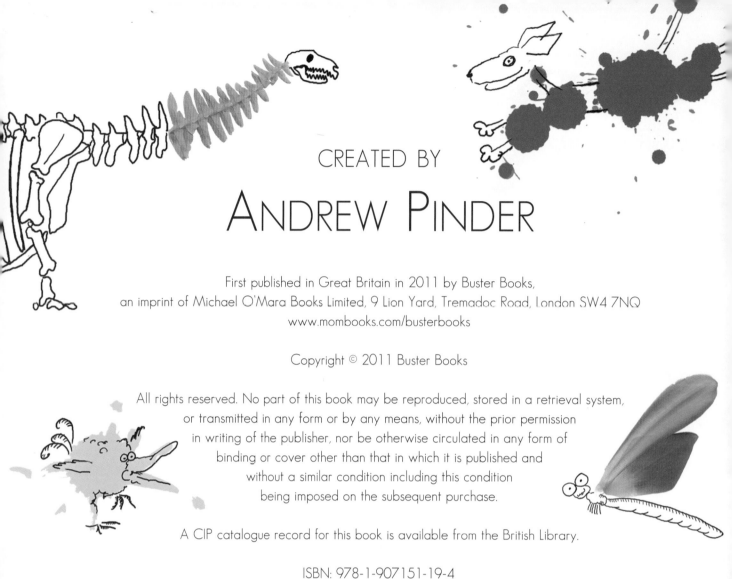

CREATED BY

ANDREW PINDER

First published in Great Britain in 2011 by Buster Books,
an imprint of Michael O'Mara Books Limited, 9 Lion Yard, Tremadoc Road, London SW4 7NQ
www.mombooks.com/busterbooks

A CIP catalogue record for this book is available from the British Library.

ISBN: 978-1-907151-19-4

2 4 6 8 10 9 7 5 3 1

Printed and bound in December 2010 by Tien Wah Press Ltd, 4 Pandan Crescent, Singapore, 128 475.

Papers used by Michael O'Mara Books are natural, recyclable products made
from wood grown in sustainable forests. The manufacturing processes
conform to the environmental regulations of the country of origin.

If you like doodling, visit our doodle website at:
www.doyoudoodle.co.uk

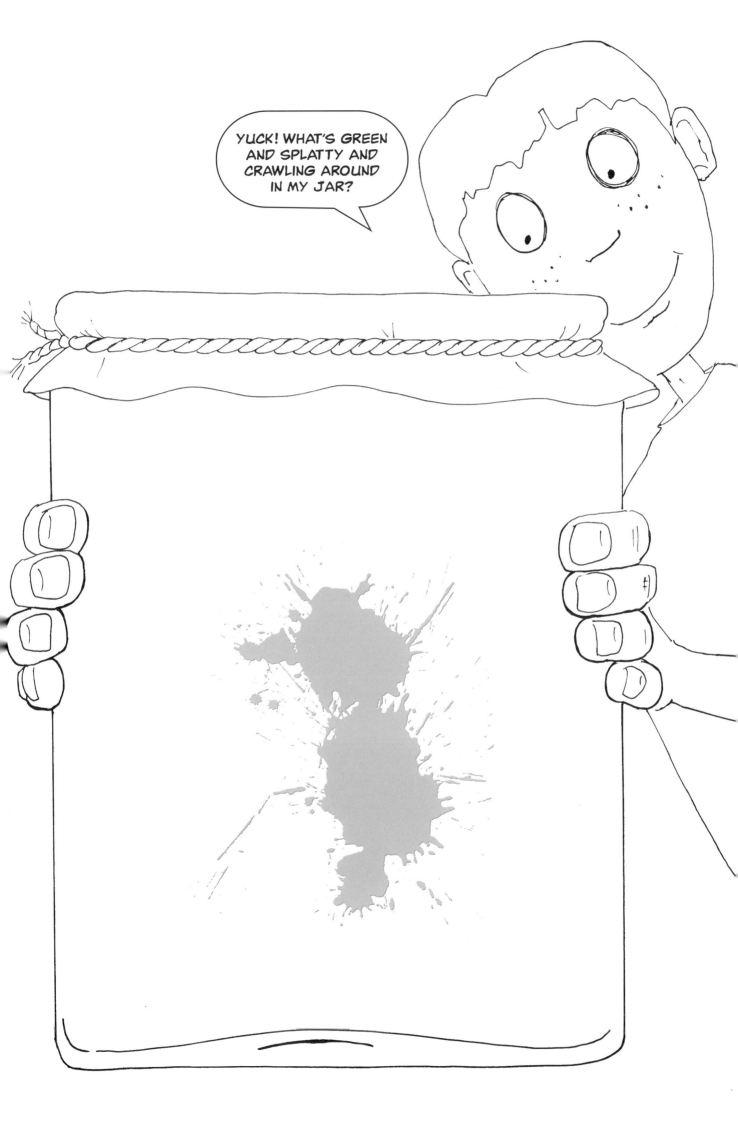

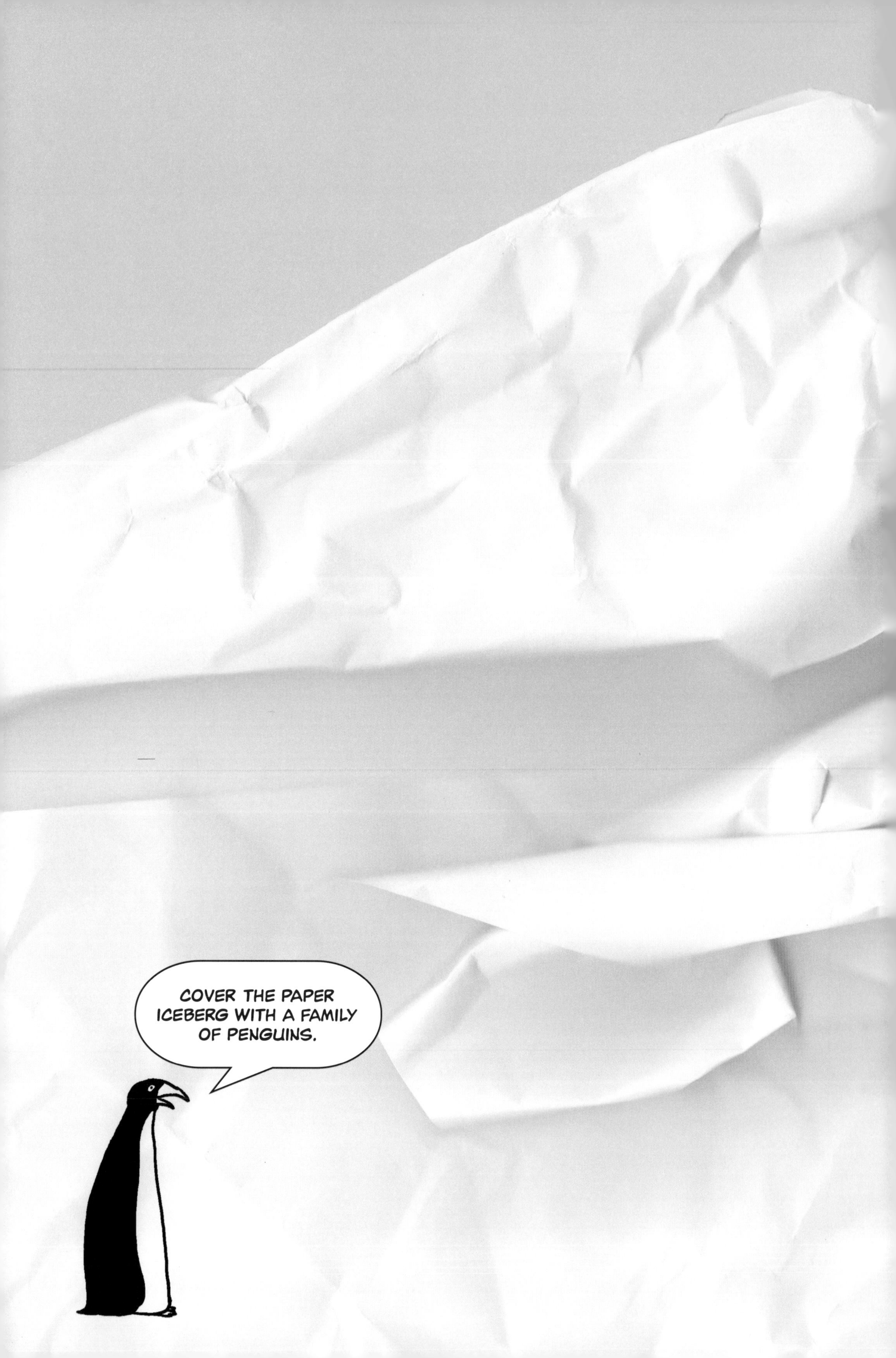
COVER THE PAPER ICEBERG WITH A FAMILY OF PENGUINS.

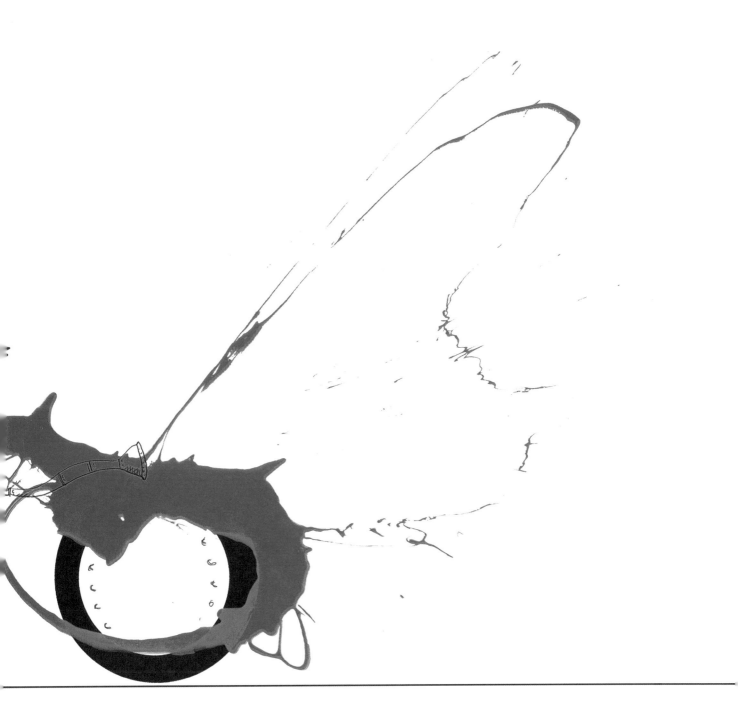

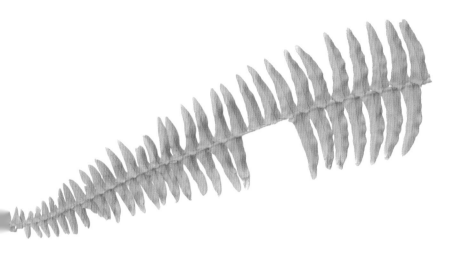
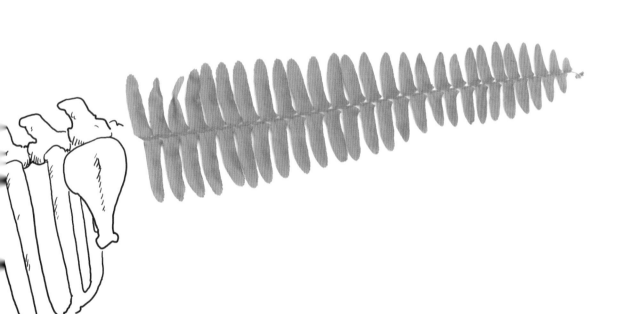

GIVE US SILLY FACES AND EVEN SILLIER NAMES.

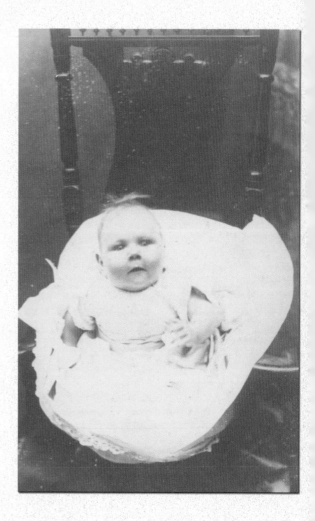

DRAW FAIRIES UNDER THE PRETTY PETAL HATS.

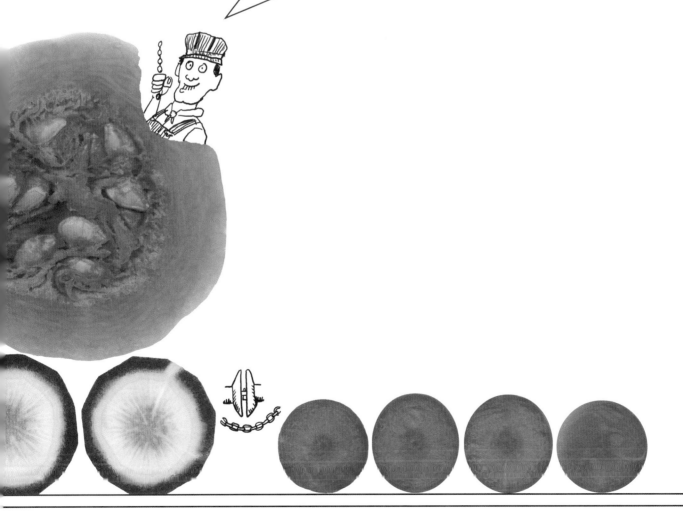

DRAW BODIES FOR THE PAINTED THUMBPRINT BUTTERFLIES.

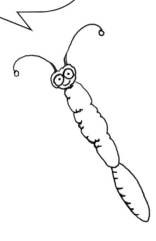

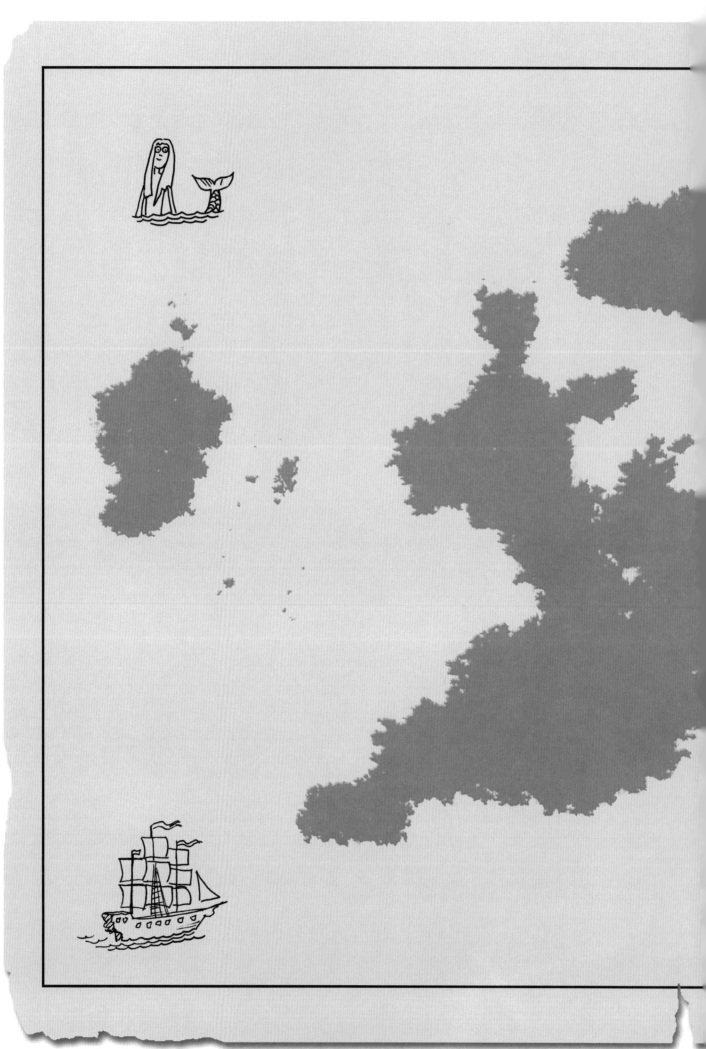

I AM A BRAINY ALIEN FROM THE PLANET CABBAGE. DRAW ME A FRIEND.

MAKE OUR PAPER
CITY A BUZZING,
BUSY PLACE
TO BE.

TURN THE
SPLATS INTO CUTE
ANIMALS, LIKE ME.

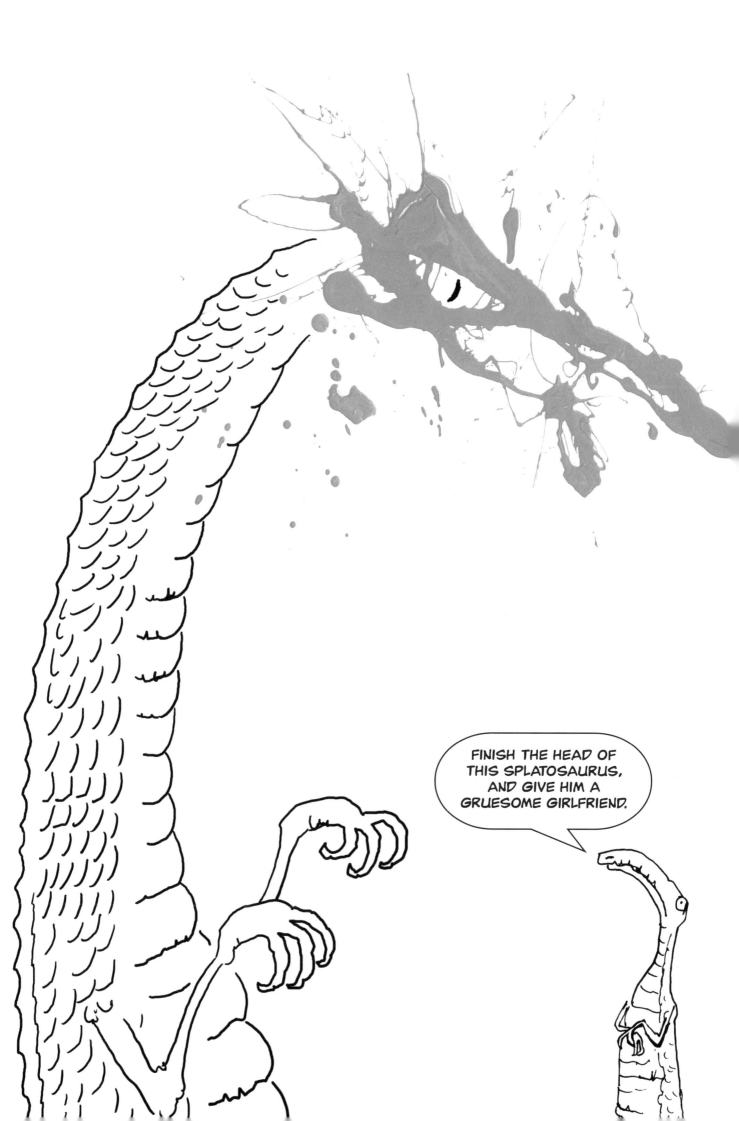

DRAW ROCKETS ON THE SPLATTER TRAILS AND ADD PLANETS IN OUTER SPACE.

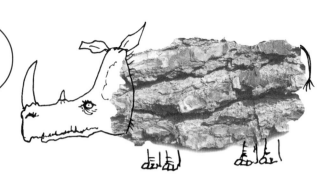

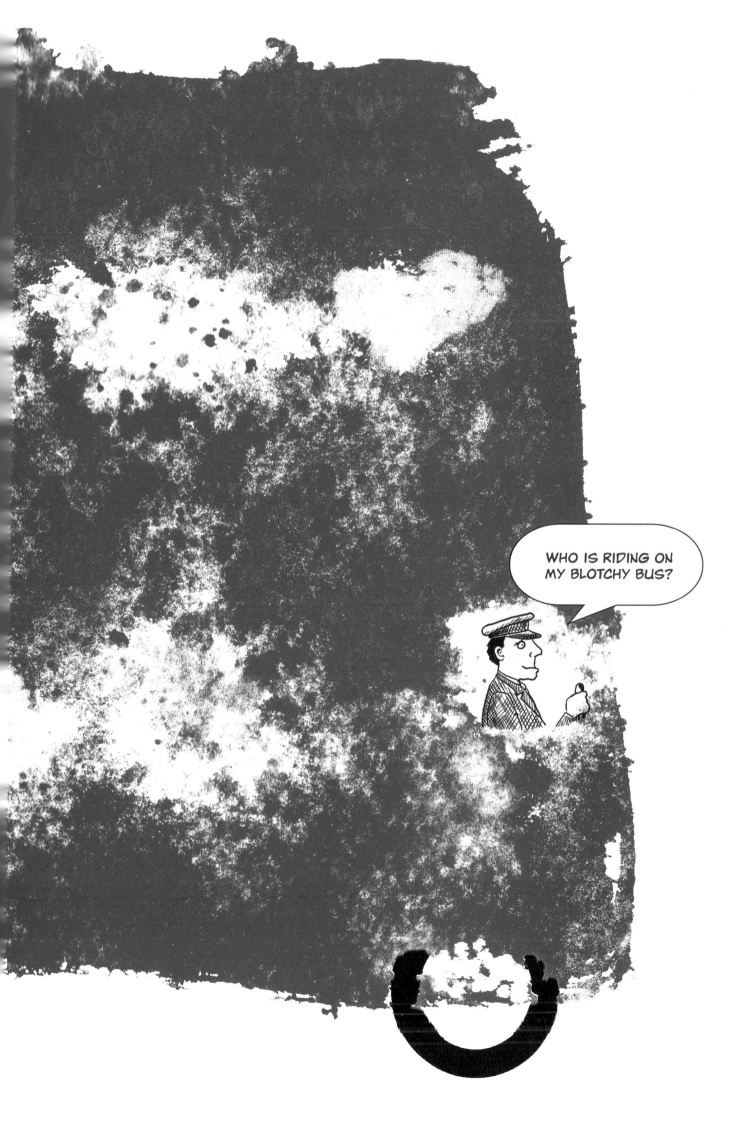

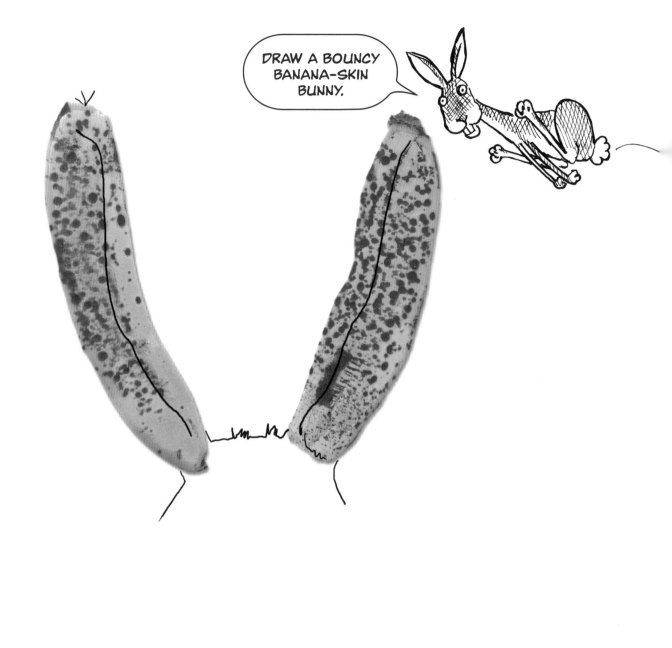

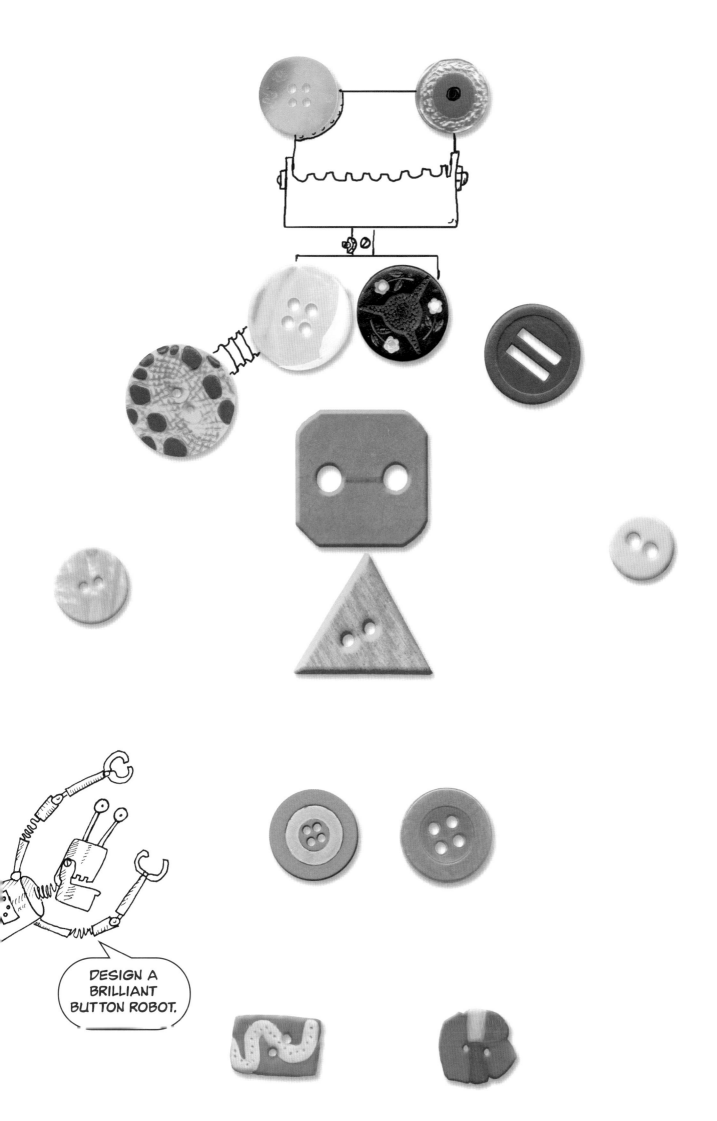

DESIGN A BRILLIANT BUTTON ROBOT.

FINISH DRAWING MY
FEATHERED FRIEND.

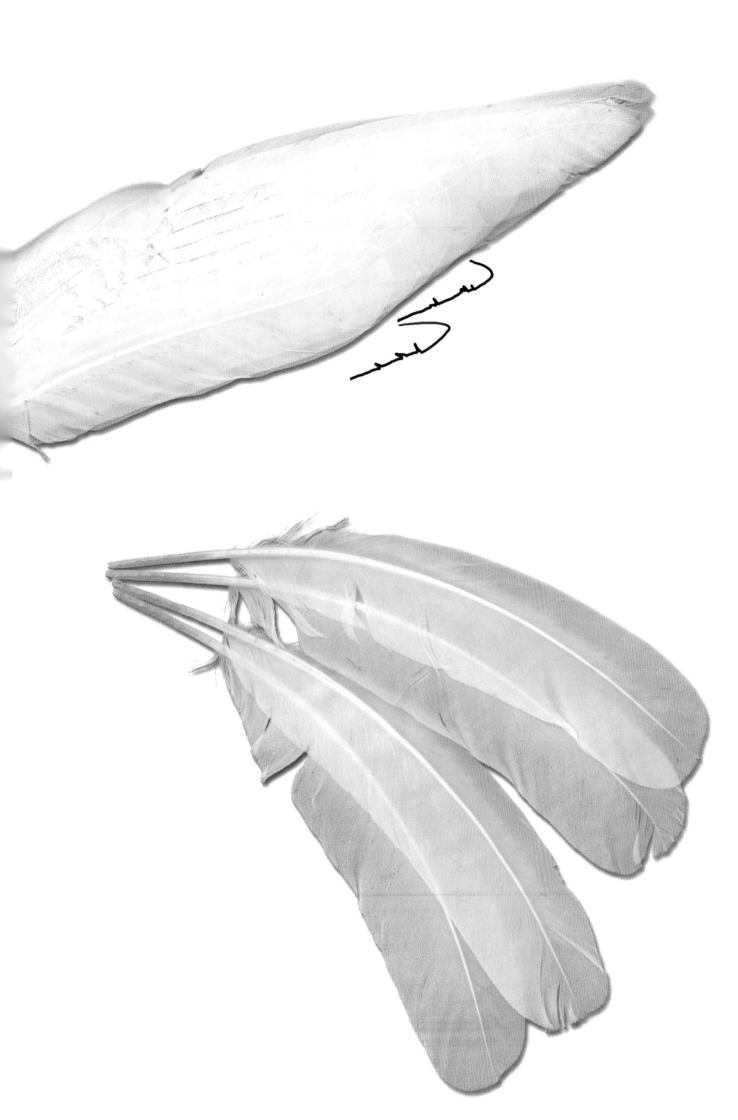

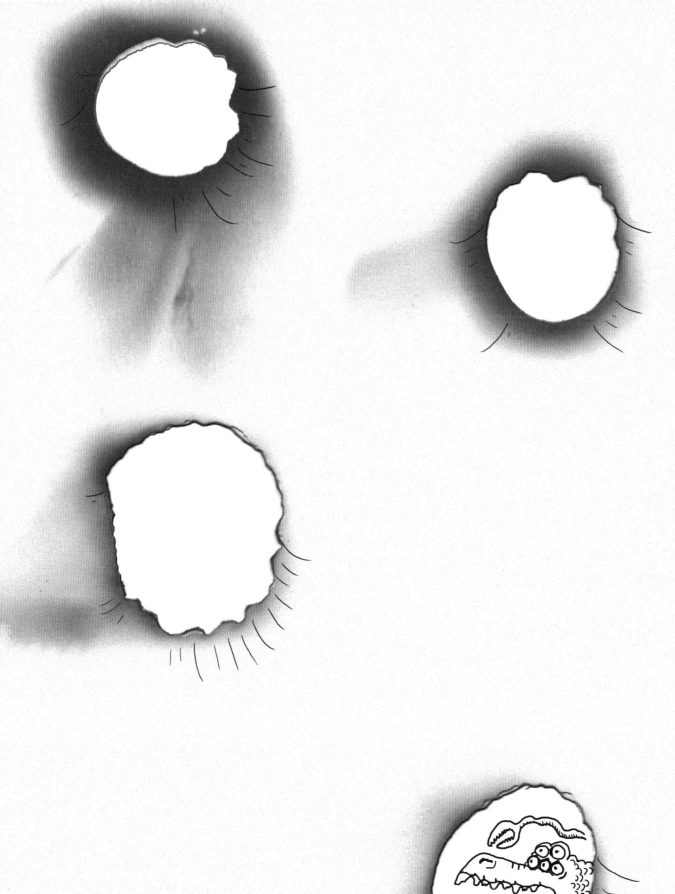

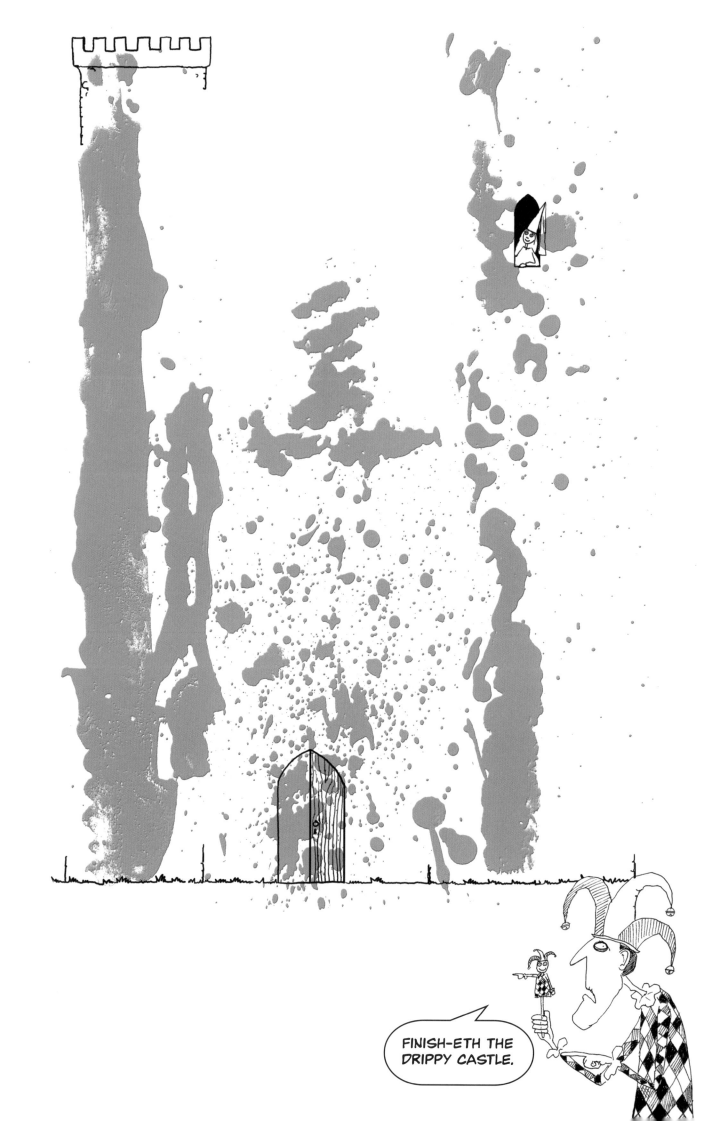

TURN THIS SPLODGE INTO A COLOURFUL CARNIVAL MASK, AND DRAW SOMEONE WEARING IT.

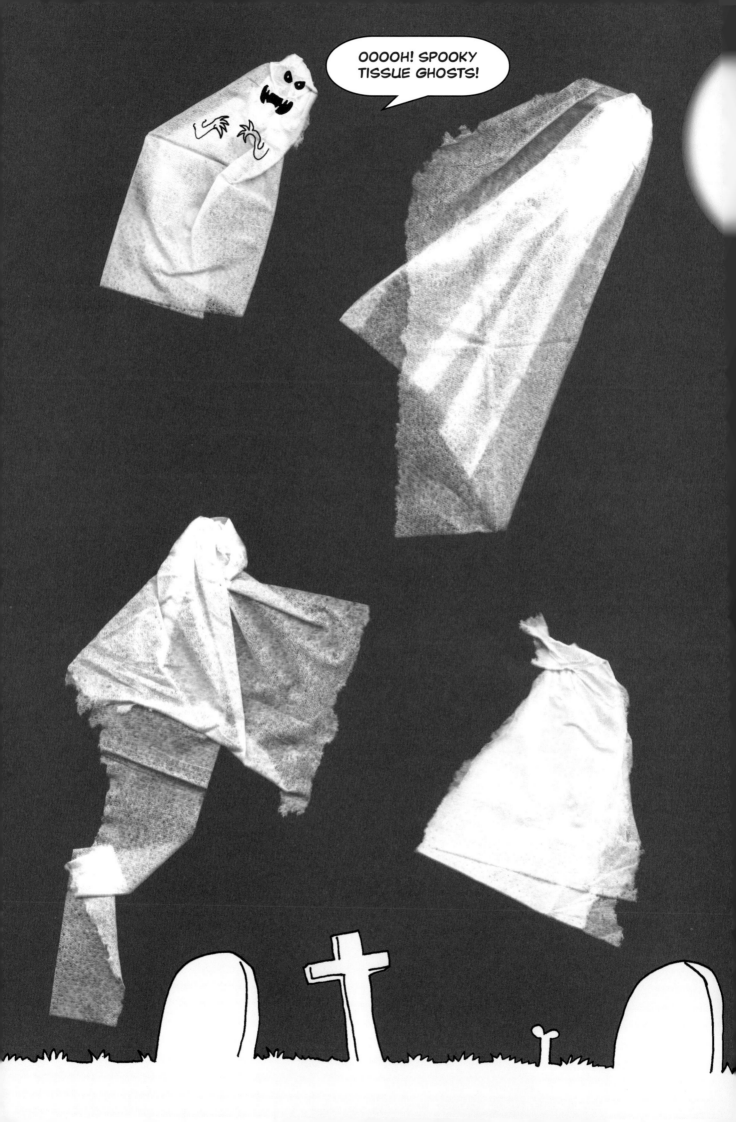

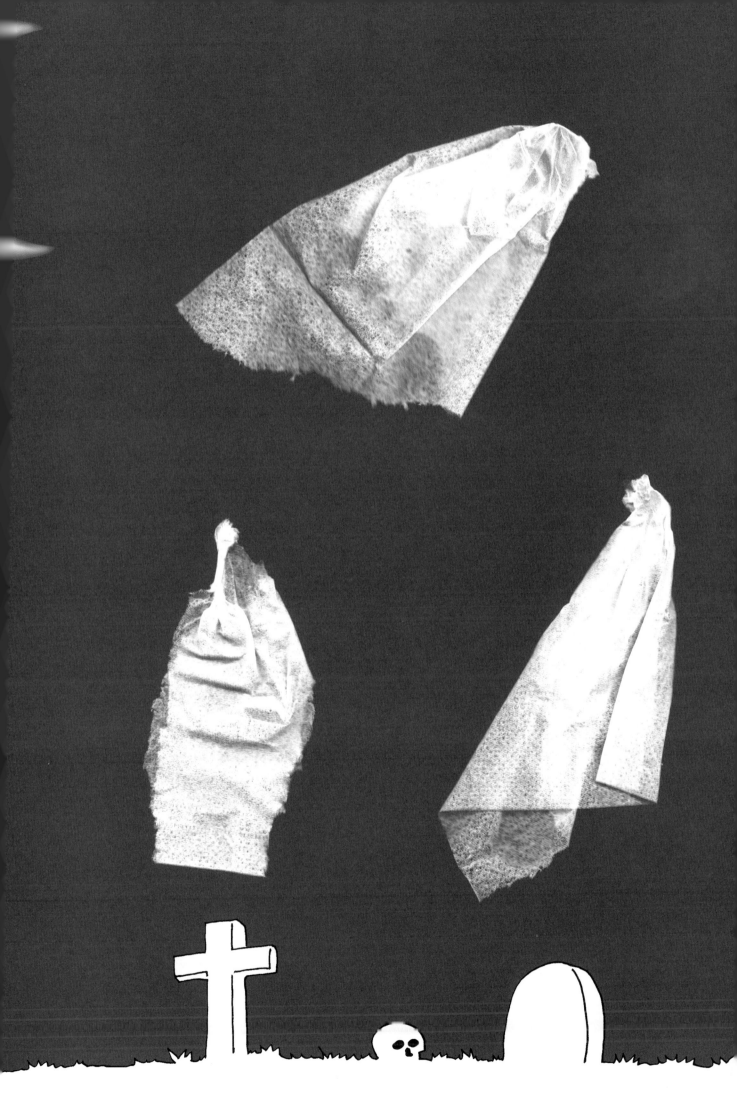

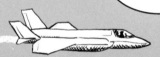

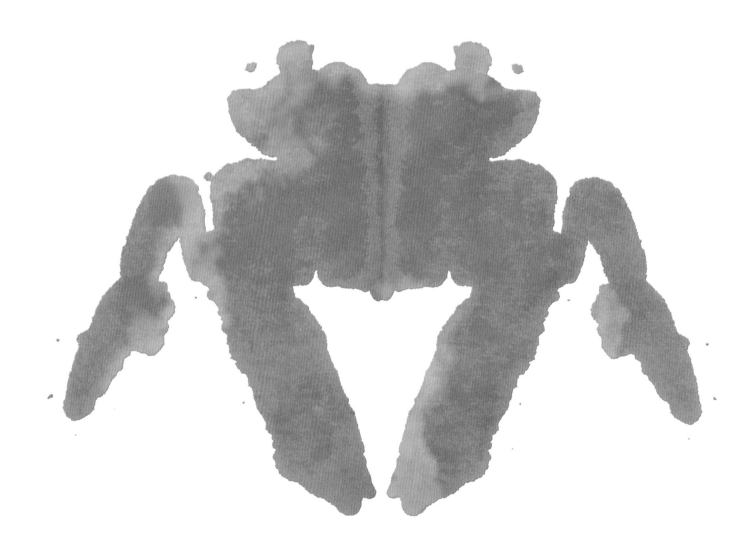

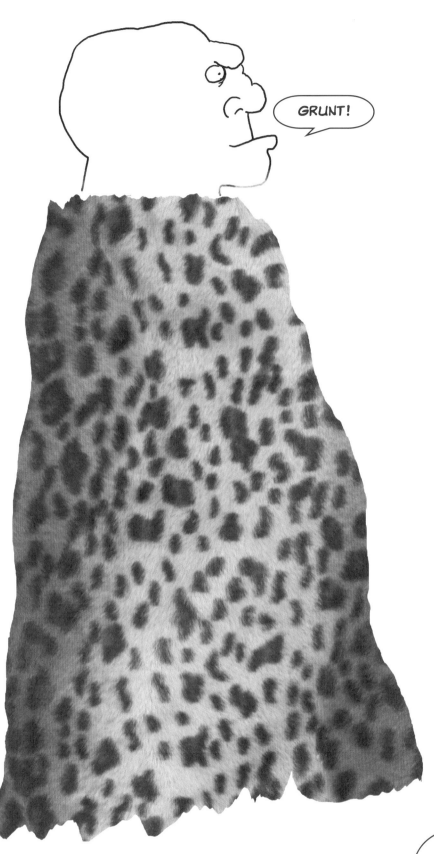

GRUNT!

FINISH THE CAVEMAN WEARING THIS LEOPARD SKIN.

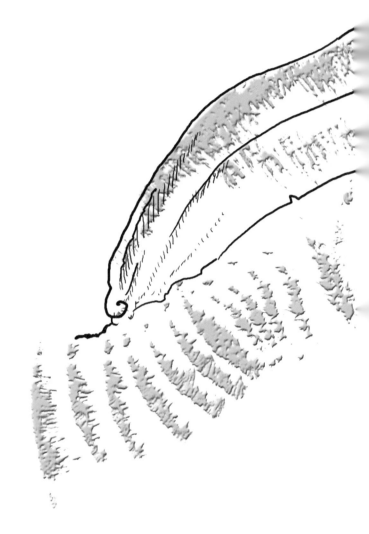

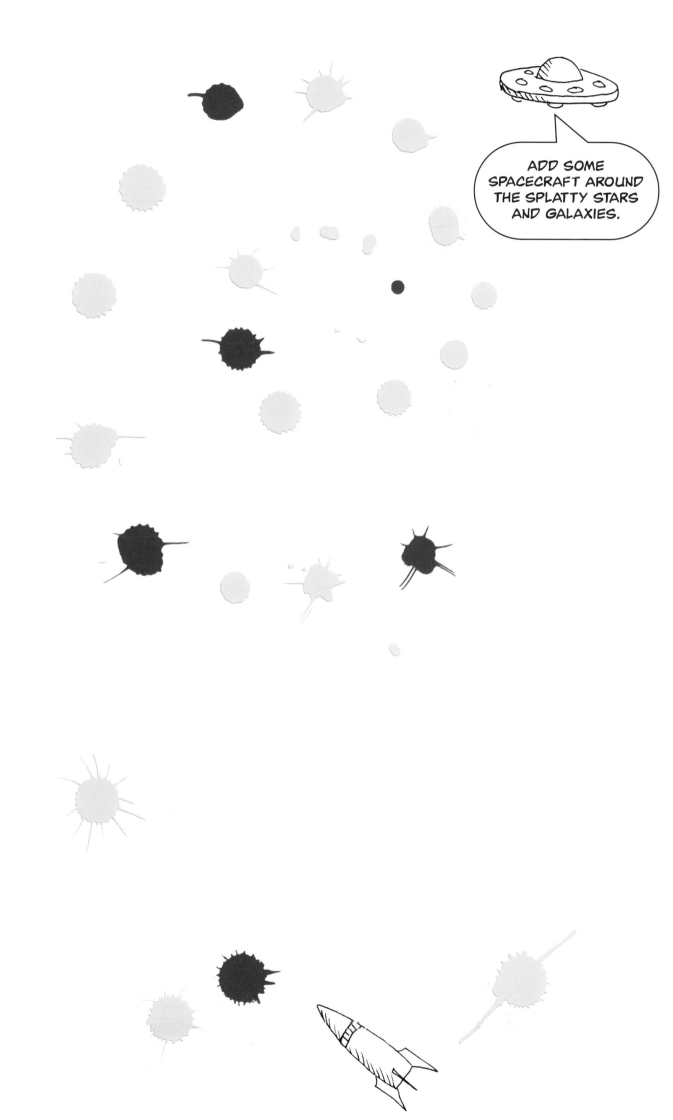

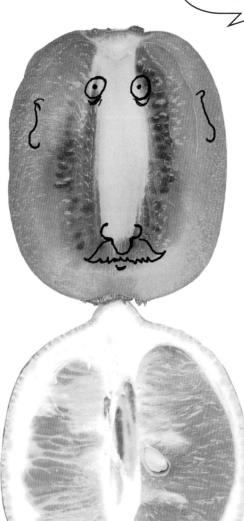
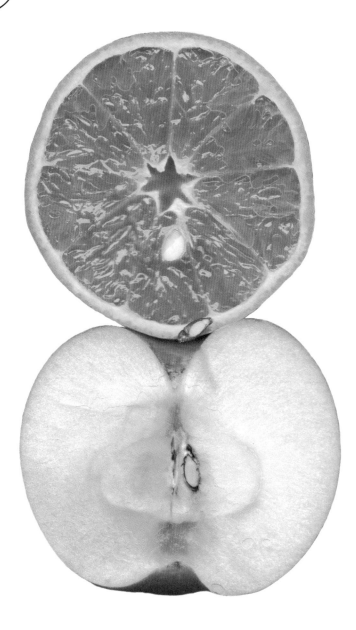

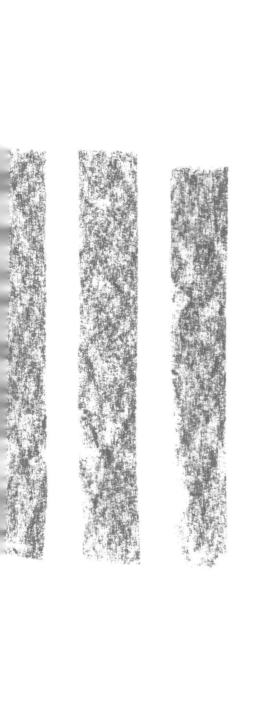

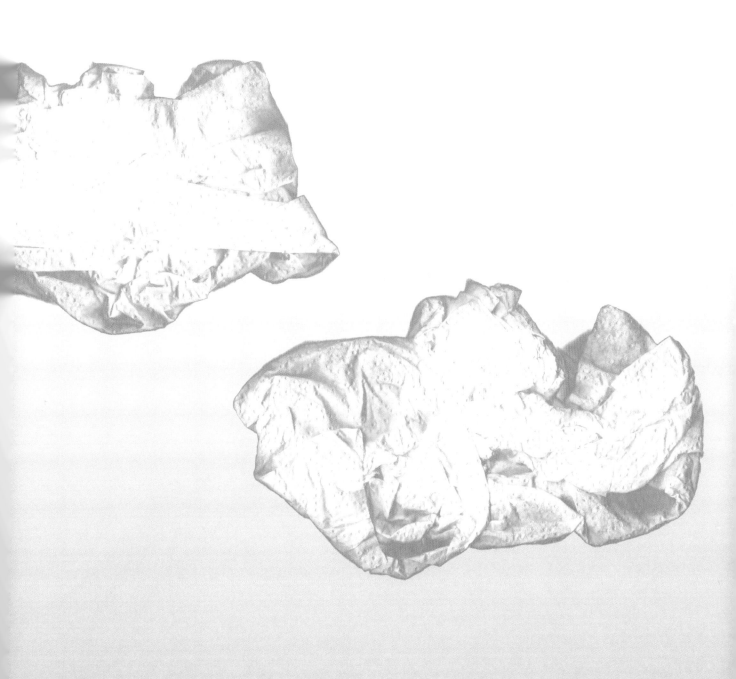

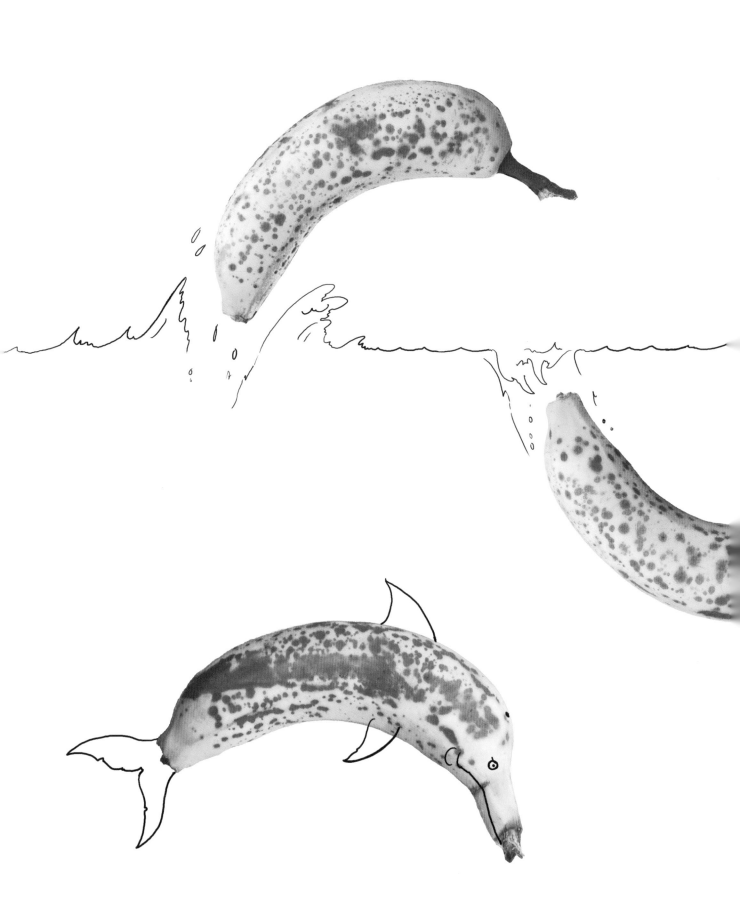

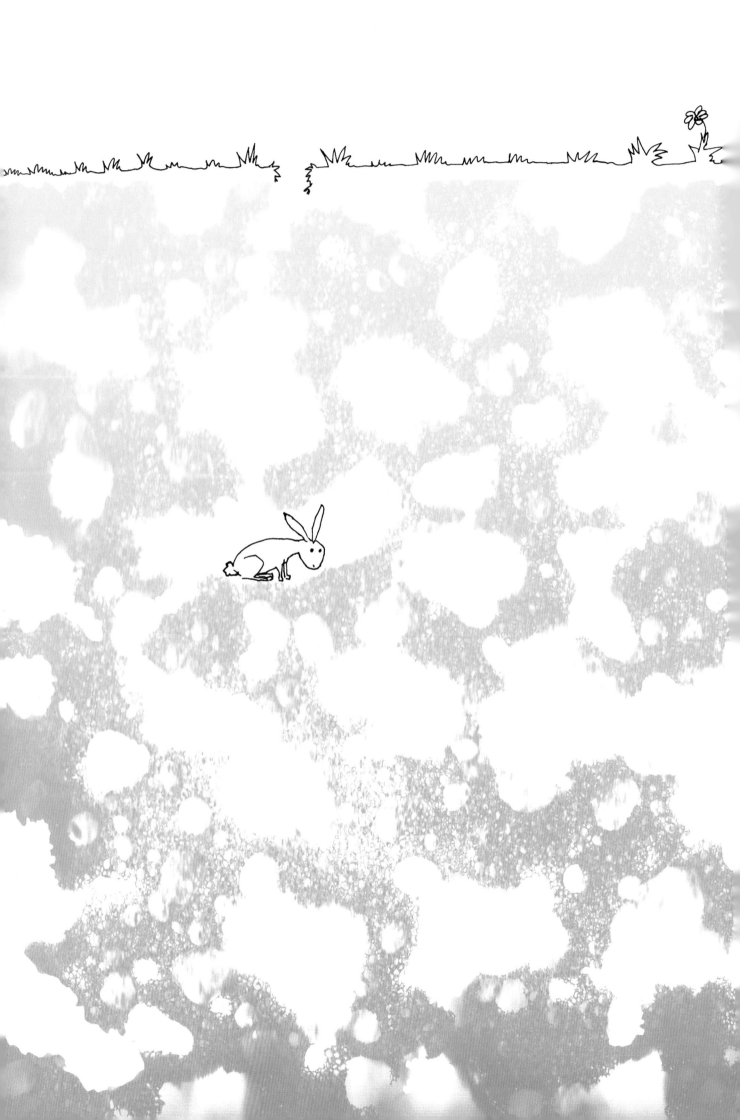

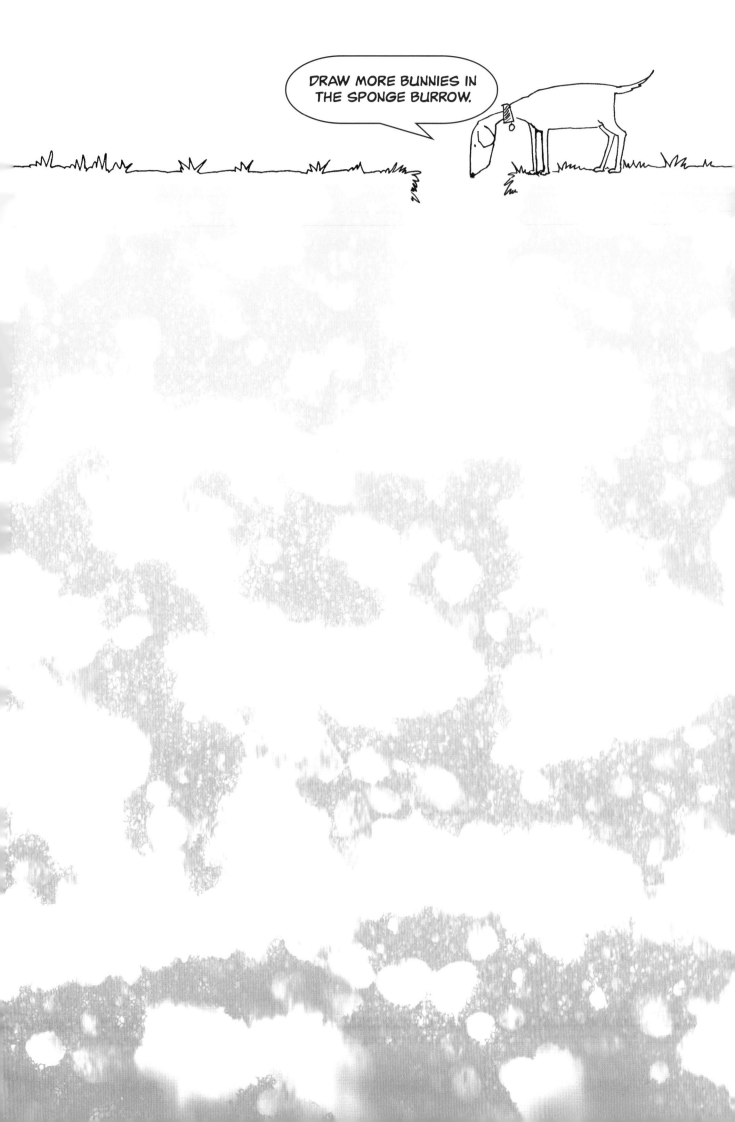

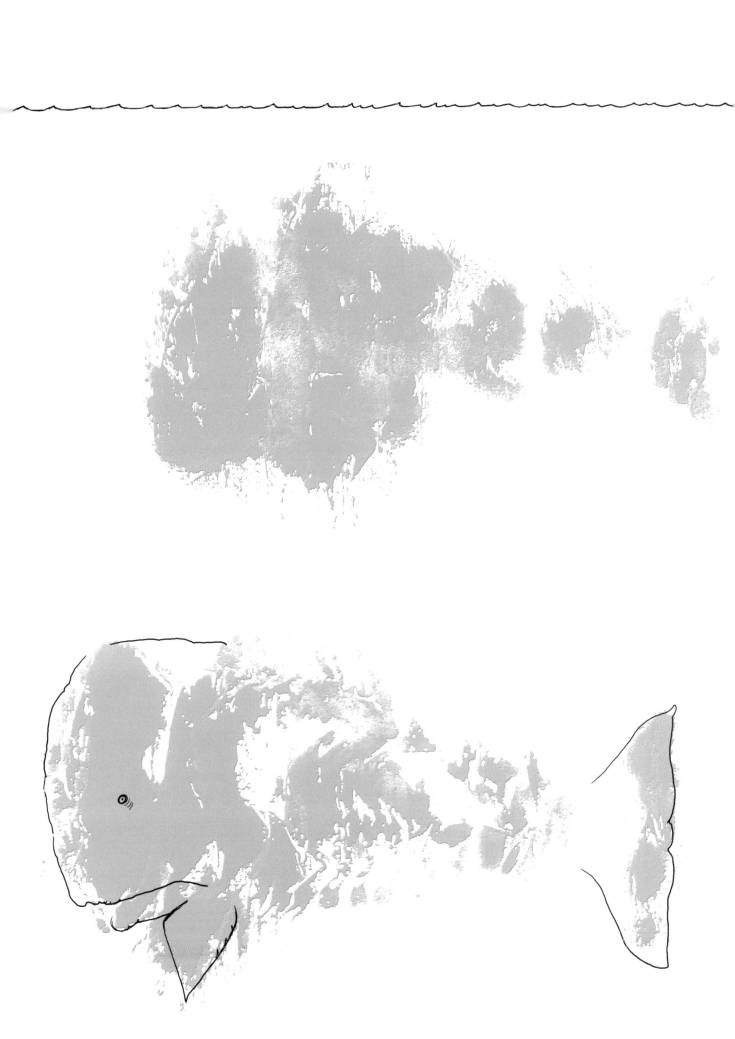

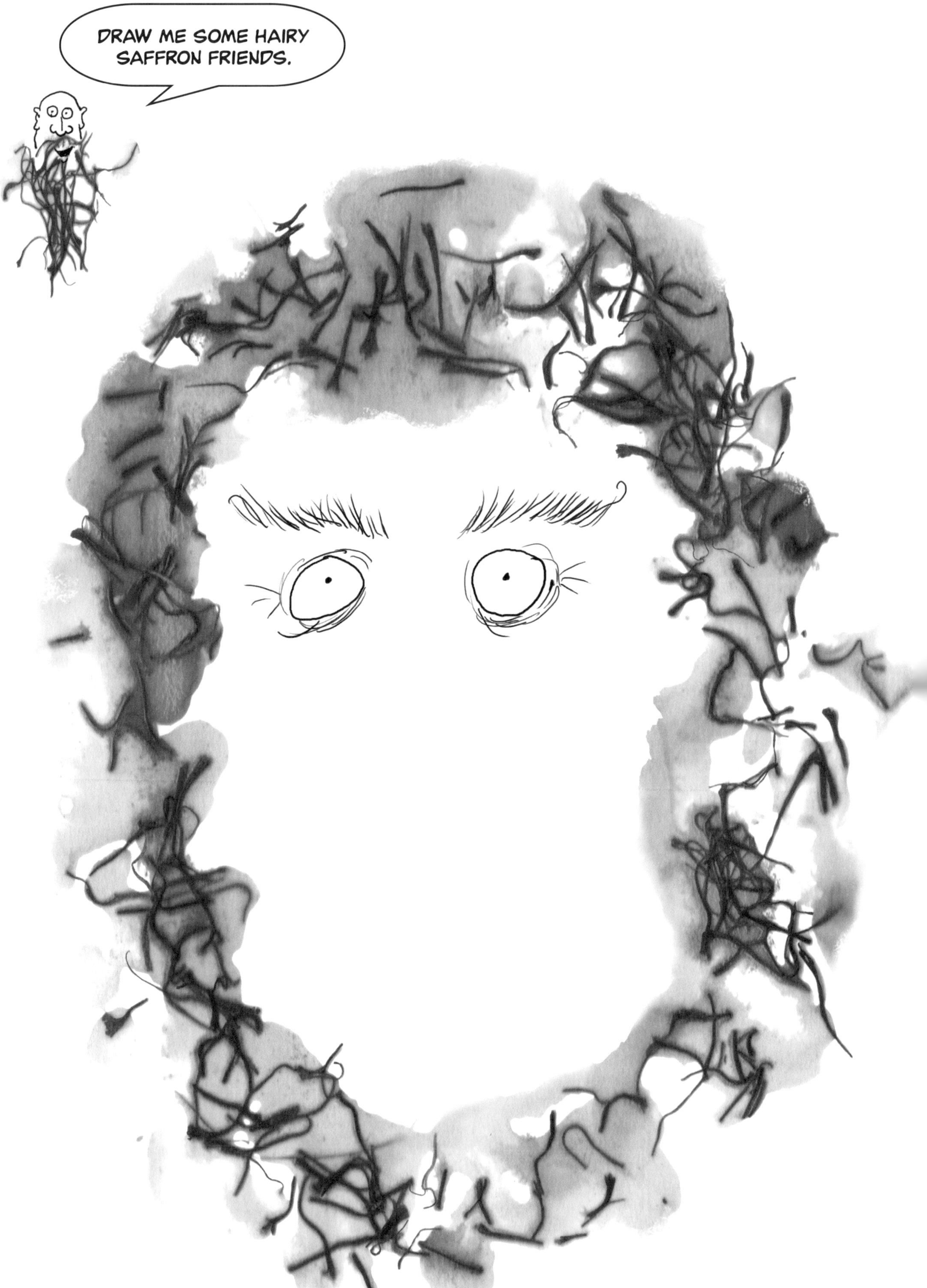
DRAW ME SOME HAIRY SAFFRON FRIENDS.

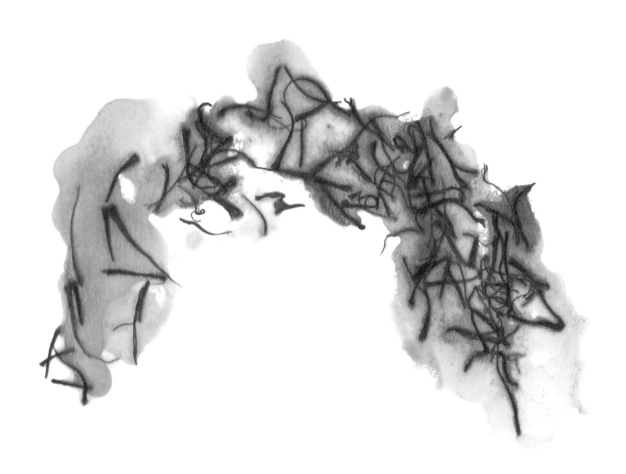

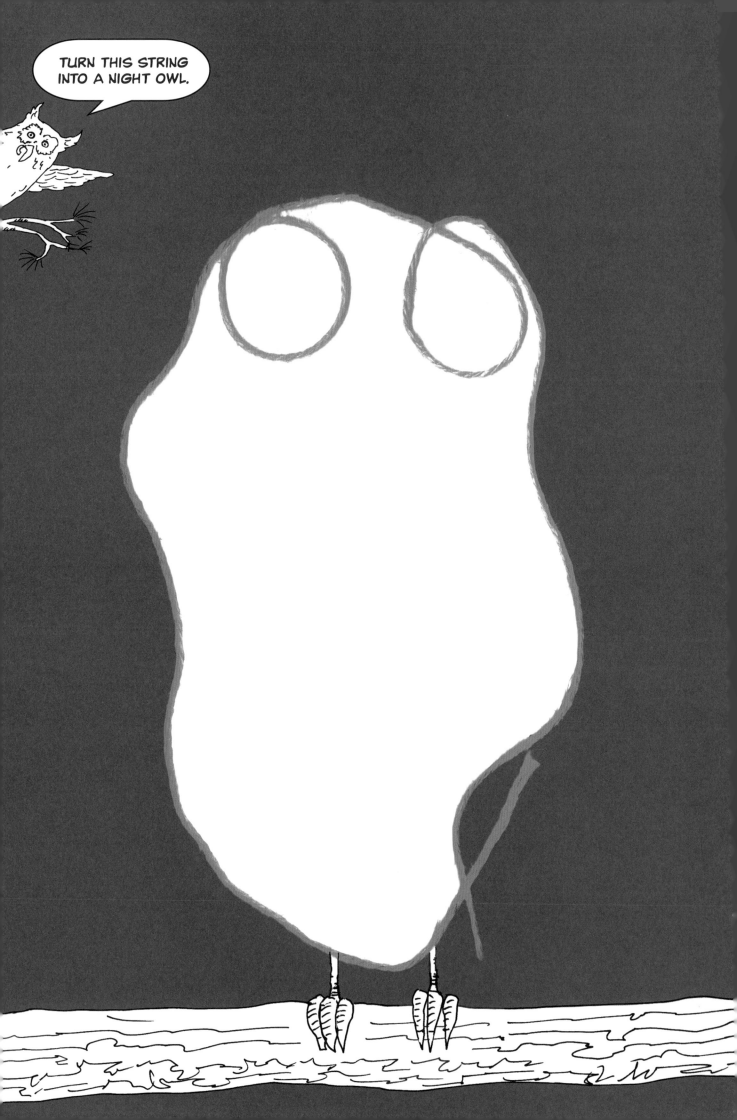

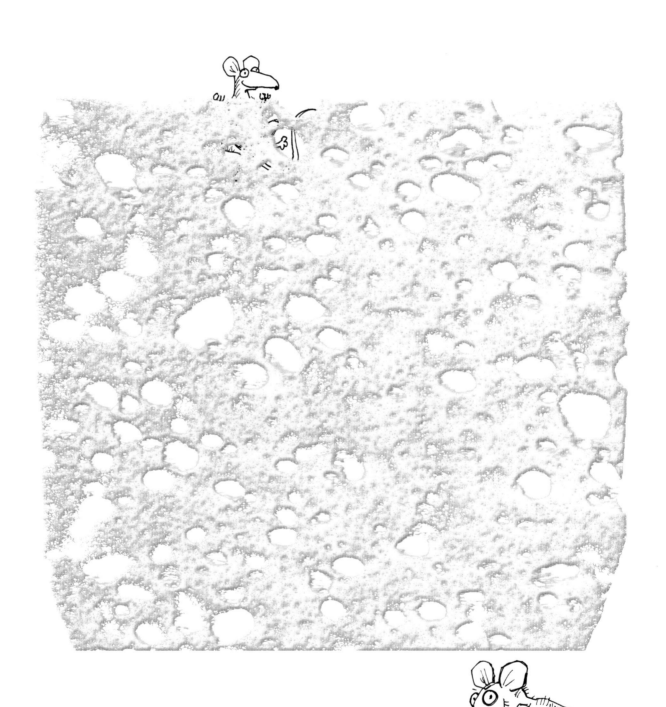

DECORATE THE CHRISTMAS TREE.

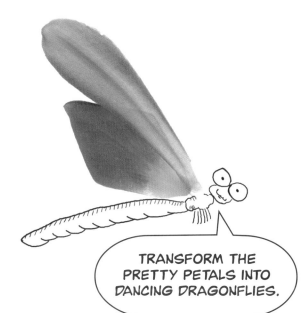

TRANSFORM THE PRETTY PETALS INTO DANCING DRAGONFLIES.

DRAW MORE PEOPLE IN OLIVE-LEAF HATS, READY TO DANCE AT THE CARNIVAL.